To my grandmothers
Herminie and Andrée.
R. F.

To my daughter.
That we may be able one day
to remember together all the
moments of happiness of
what is now our present.
T. L.

Angela
and the
cherry tree

Raphaële Frier

Teresa Lima

BERBAY
PUBLISHING

Once again, Angela got up before daybreak.

At this hour, all is calm.
This is the hour that smells of fresh grass
when you open the window.
This is the hour when drops of water
glisten on flower stems in the garden.

Angela fills her cup with milk.

She adds a drop of coffee,
tracing light brown swirls
on the white surface.

Then the swirls disappear
and the white becomes darker.

The rooster has woken the neighbours' dogs:
morning has broken.

Maybe she'll come today.
That would be good.

Angela decides to change the water in the vase.
That will be good for the flowers.
They may even last a few more days.

Then she goes into the bathroom
and splashes water on her face.
She takes care with her hair,
spraying it with perfume.

She smells good. She is beautiful.
And she is full of hope.

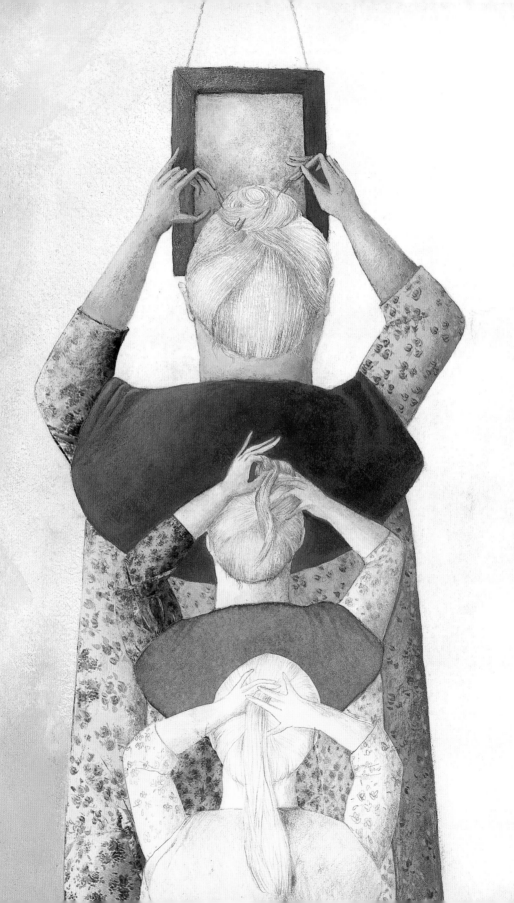

The big hand on the clock
has not gone round very far.
It's still too early.
Angela has time.

She gets out the packet of flour,
the butter dish and the sugar.

She takes off the ring she wears on her finger
and starts mashing the butter into the white flour.

It's all sticky and slippery
and she gets it everywhere.

Now a lovely sweet smell
fills the house.

It smells of shortbread cookies,
Angela's speciality.

She has been mad about them
since she was a little girl.

That's why she makes them so often.

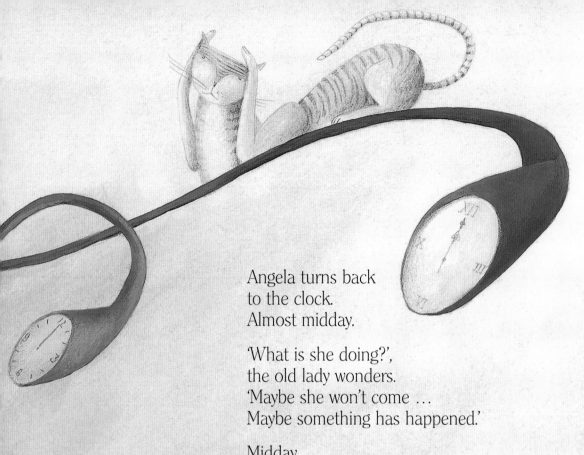

Angela turns back
to the clock.
Almost midday.

'What is she doing?',
the old lady wonders.
'Maybe she won't come …
Maybe something has happened.'

Midday.
It's the hour when Angela
finds it harder to be hopeful.

Every times she sees
those two hands of the clock,
one on top of the other,
she becomes upset and anxious.
What if her visitor
were never to come again?

What if, from now on,
she were to have nothing more for company
than her own sick, old bones?

And now a storm has come
up inside Angela.

Her heart is lurching in all directions,
losing its balance, bumping into things.
It feels like it's going over the edge.

To get relief from this torment,
Angela turns on the TV.
She sits down in her armchair
and begins sorting the letters
that appear on the screen.

She loves this game show.

B – X – R – S – A – E – S

She is looking for words and
thinking out loud:
'Bases, bars, bras, brass, axes …
ASSBREX!'

That's when she hears a small voice
behind her crying:

'Bravo, Angela! Seven letters, you win!'

'Ah, there you are!', the old lady replies.
'You took your time, didn't you!
I was getting worried.'

'Angela, there's a fantastic smell in the house.
I'm guessing it's those shortbread cookies I adore.'

'Well yes, I told you I was expecting you.
Have a look in the oven …'

'Yum, we're in for a treat!
I'll arrange them on this plate,
then we'll put it on the table.

I'll have a glass of milk.
Do you have any in your fridge?
I'll pour some milk into a large cup for you,
just as you like it, then I'll add a drop of coffee, eh?'

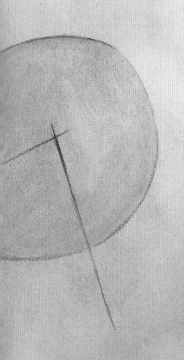

Angela is happy.

She is eating her favourite cookies
with the little girl she was waiting for
with such longing.

She feels light, she feels calm.
The small icy shivers
once imprisoned under her dress
have disappeared.

The clock can do whatever it likes
with its hands.
It can put one on top of the other
or keep them far apart.
Angela doesn't care,
she is at peace.

'Angela,' cries the little one,
her mouth still full of shortbread.
'Can we go out to the garden?'
'If you want to,' replies the old lady.

'Hey, wait for me! You know
I can't walk down that path
all by myself.'

'Coming!' cries the little one,
and she comes running back.
'Don't worry Angela, I'll hold your arm.
You're not going to fall.'

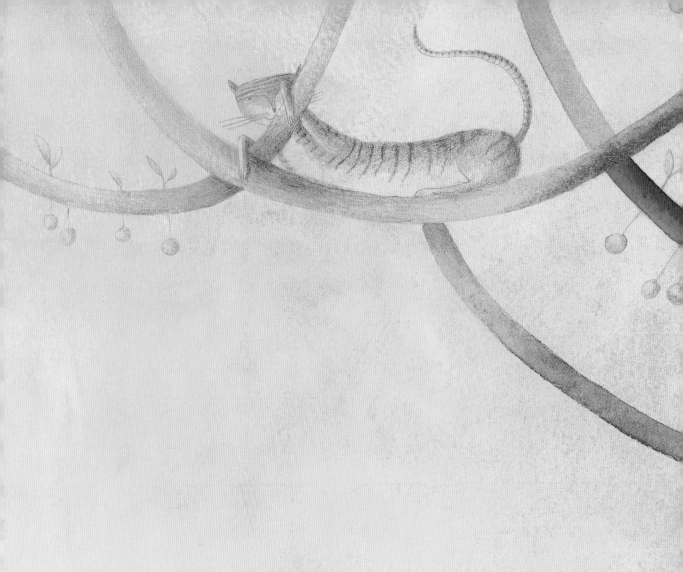

The old lady walks with difficulty,
but allows herself to be led
down to the big cherry tree.

Above her, perched in the branches
that hang with pink pearls of fruit,
the little one fills her basket,
fills her mouth and fills Angela's heart,
there under the cherry tree.

'Wow, they're so juicy!
Angela, your cherries are so sweet!
We can't just leave them for the birds.
They're for us. We're going to eat them
And make cherry desserts.'

Angela's tired heart
beats under the branches
of the big cherry tree.

'And snails!' exclaims the child.
'It rained last night.
The irises must be full of snails.

Come on, Angela,
let's go and see if we can find some.
And this time,
the first one will be for you.'

The old lady moves with great difficulty,
but she lets herself be led
to the row of blue flowers
growing along the wall of the house.

'Oh, that one's a beauty, look!'

Angela's tired heart
beats above the blue flowers
growing along the garden path.

At that moment,
John pushes open the gate.
He comes nearly every day
at the same time.

He sees straight away that
something is wrong.
The old lady is alone in her garden,
and the white collar of her dress
is stained with pink.

On the back of her hand
there is a snail with its feelers out.
She seems to be having fun.
She is laughing and talking to someone
who doesn't exist.

'Mum …?'

The old lady doesn't reply.

'Mum?'

Angela hasn't heard his voice.
She is busy tickling the feelers
of her little friend in its shell.

The feelers come up … whoa! … they go down,
they come up … whoa! … they go down.

And then she turns because she senses
a very sweet presence quite close to her.

She raises her head, the snail lowers its feelers.

Above her there is John, with his shining eyes
and his loving smile.
He enfolds Angela in his big arms.
Angela's tired heart
beats against John's chest.

'Daddy?'

'No Mum, it's me.
What are you doing in the garden?
You didn't come out here by yourself, did you?

'The little one helped me,' replied the old lady.
'She came today and we ate some cookies.
There are some left over. Would you like one?'

Now John thinks
the little one is really fantastic.
He takes Angela by the arm
and helps her sit on the
swinging garden seat.

He whispers in her ear,
'Don't move, just stay here
till I get back.'

Angela does as she's told.
She waits and she swings.

John reappears
with a book in his hand.

'Let me sit down next to you.
That way you'll see better.'

Side by side
on the swinging garden seat
they turn the pages they know and love.

'Look at that! You remember,
the cherry tree had just been planted …'